Just Dessert

Polly Powell

Harcourt Brace & Company
San Diego New York London

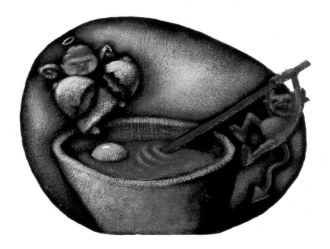

Requests for permission to make copies of any part of the work should be
mailed to: Permissions Department, Harcourt Brace & Company,
6277 Sea Harbor Drive, Orlando, Florida 32887-6777.

Library of Congress Cataloging-in-Publication Data
Powell, Polly, 1962-
Just dessert/Polly Powell.—1st ed.
p.   cm.
Summary: While sneaking to the kitchen at midnight to get the last piece
of Super Yellow Cake with Fudge Frosting, young Patsy is frightened by a series of household
objects and sounds made monstrous by her imagination.
ISBN 0-15-200383-5
[1. Imagination—Fiction. 2. Night—Fiction. 3. Fear—Fiction.]
I. Title
PZ7.P87775Ju 1996
[E]—dc20   94-48360

First edition
A B C D E

Printed in Singapore

The illustrations in this book were done in acrylic paint,
oil paint, and charcoal on illustration board with gesso.
The display type and the text type were
hand-lettered by the illustrator.
Color separations by Bright Arts, Ltd., Singapore
Printed and bound by Tien Wah Press, Singapore
This book was printed with soya-based inks on Leykam recycled paper,
which contains more than 20 percent postconsumer waste
and has a total recycled content of at least 50 percent.
Production supervision by Warren Wallerstein
and David Hough

To my folks,
who could never
keep the cake hidden
from me

The Apple family had swallowed the salad, finished the fish,

and devoured dessert when Patsy, the youngest Apple, expressed a desire for the remainder of the Super Yellow Cake with Fudge Frosting.

Mrs. Apple, however, said,

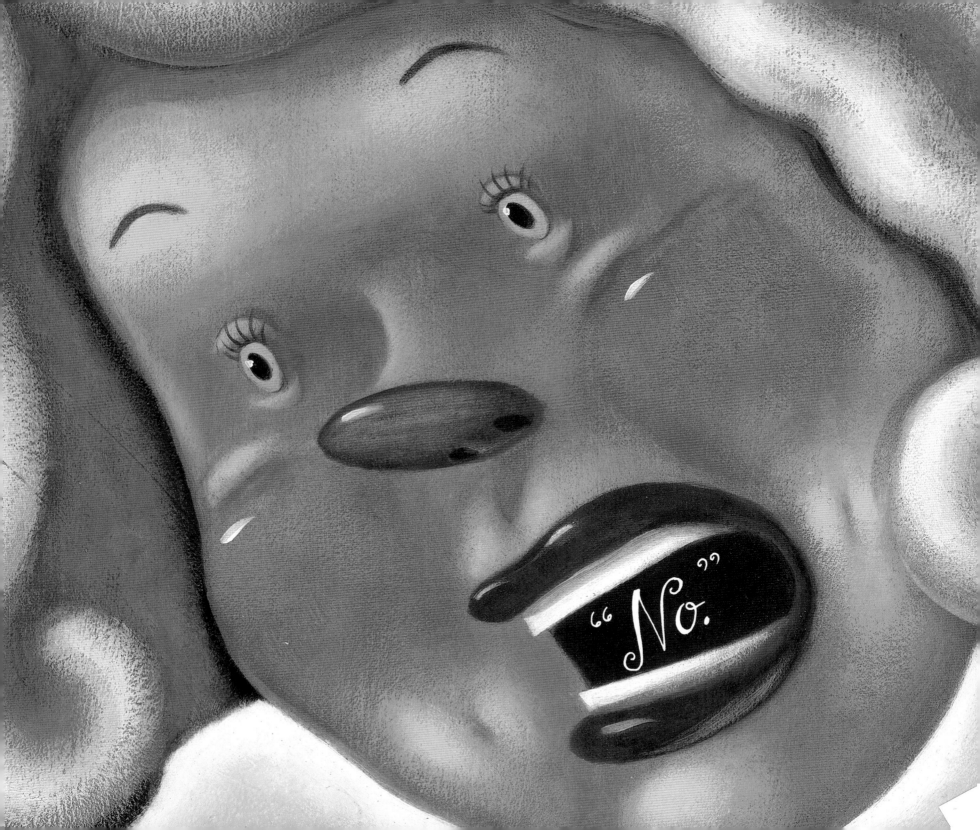

All evening long,

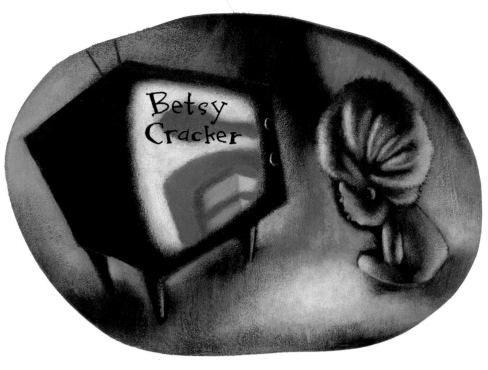

Patsy was rather preoccupied with that cake.

So late that night,

after everyone was asleep, she slunk
out of bed and boldly began the long,
dark journey to the refrigerator.

BUT

just as Patsy passed her closet door, she spotted something...

(She was
out of that room
in a hurry!)

Patsy's heart pounded.
Only the thought of that cake
kept her going. She tiptoed down
the hallway and that's when she heard
the noise....

It sounded like
a
GREAT
BIG
Grumbling
GROWLING

(DID
I MENTION
GRUMPY?)

GRIZZLY BEAR!

(Not wishing to
meet a grizzly bear face·to·face,
Patsy darted downstairs.)

But in the living room, she jumped when she saw a clinky, clattery...

(Patsy moved her own bones straight into the laundry room.)

There she gaped at a ghastly, GRINNING . . .

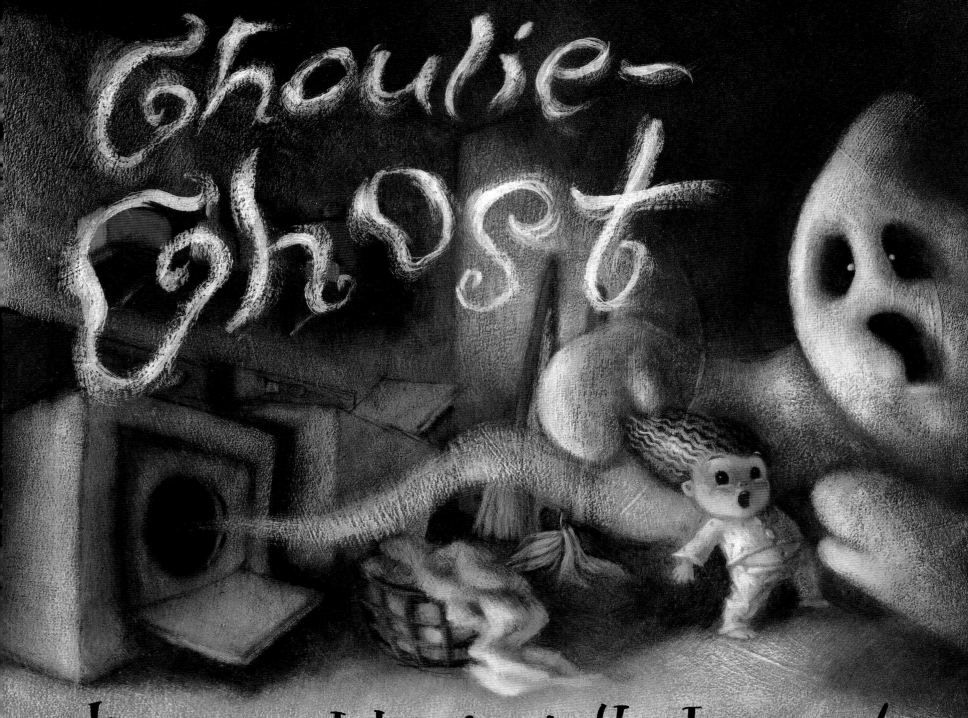

Ghoulie-Ghost

dipping and dancing in the doorway!

(Once, when it dipped left, Patsy dodged right.)

At last
Patsy reached
the refrigerator.
She snatched the
Super Yellow Cake with
Fudge Frosting
and began the long
journey back to
her bedroom.

Patsy closed her eyes tight as she slipped past

the ghoulie·ghost.

She looked the other way as she sprinted past the Skeleton~Man.

She hummed aloud as she hurried past the grumbling, growling grizzly bear.

And she scurried past the monstrous thing in the closet just as fast as she could.

But there
in her bedroom,
Patsy suddenly saw under
her bed a
slinky, slithery

Patsy's
only choice
was to take a running
leap under the covers.

There was just one thing she forgot,

The end